WHERE FISH CAN BREATHE

TRICIA D. WAGNER

LYRIDAE BOOKS

PRAISE FOR TRICIA D. WAGNER

*I begin to sing about Poseidon, the great god, mover of the earth and fruitless
sea, god of the deep who is also lord of Helicon and wide Aegae.
A two-fold office the gods allotted you, O Shaker of the Earth,
to be a tamer of horses and a savior of ships!*

Homer

WHERE FISH CAN BREATHE

T he first time Swift's father, Justus, took him sailing on the North Atlantic, compelled by a ferocious father-love, he schooled Swift on the many ways boys could be killed by water and wind.

Justus taught his lad that he must hang on for life and limb when the sailboat was cruising over the water.

And now, hang on Swift did, because his brother Trystan was at the helm.

Trystan punched the auxiliary and raced the wind toward a silver sunset, rocketing their father's boat across the sea, eluding its sucking tug when he was with the current, soaring over frothy peaks, then heaving through the waves when he opposed their draw, swooping up vertical climbs and rushing down glossy slopes.

Thin as a jackstaff and only ten, Swift braced himself against the wind. Face to face with the North Atlantic, he couldn't breathe. To breathe, he had to buck his head below the gale. But he could never stay down long. Down would only show him his bare feet, while up, oh up—up would show him water waves coursing in measured fits, heaving against the bow of his father's sailboat, arcing into the salty wind like the shining backs of a school of leviathans.

The North Atlantic wind could slice through sails like a razor (Swift had seen it).

It could knock seasoned sailors off their sea legs with the flat of its steely side, and with one mighty swipe, it could cast boys from the safety of their boats to oblivion.

There was nothing to be done about the North Atlantic's raging, because his father's sport fishing boat was far away—lost, maybe (Swift hoped)—in the Giotto-blue abyss, distantly north of his island shire.

Swift had been on the boat with his father and brothers many times before, but never for night fishing.

The chemical high of the flight through waves was a rush, but it paled in comparison with the thrill of being on the sailboat overnight, as one of the men.

The youngest of the four brothers, younger than the rest by a decade or more, Swift had always been 'the lad,' and though he was tall for ten, and growing fast, he felt of a different species from the muscled men who shared his home.

In the past, Swift contributed little more than wild play to the fishing expeditions.

He'd haunt the decks, and get in the way, and retch over the rail, and ask too many questions, and Justus hadn't wanted him to come on this one.

Night fishing was a man's sport, Swift overheard Justus tell their mum. The North Sea was capricious, and a night fishing trip on treacherous waters was no place for the lad.

Swift had burst in and begged to go and promised his father that this time he'd be different and would handle the North Atlantic like a man.

And now, here he was, high on the bow, balancing like a figurehead on a galleon ship, handling the waves and weather as well as any of his brothers.

The bluster grazed him like it was the falchion blade whirled over the head of a baleful god of seas. He straightened, taking the full strike of the tempest like a man.

Standing behind him on the deck, Justus was certainly marveling at his lad.

Swift threw back his head and howled a howl wild enough to beat through the whipping wind, and loud enough to outplay the clamorous strike of waves against wood, and brash enough to reach his father's ears.

Justus' hearty laughter filled the wind.

Swift shivered for the bliss of hearing that laugh.

He absently rubbed at a sore stripe on the front of his ribs, red with irritation where the gritty spray refused to let his sunburn cool.

But he thought little of it because Trystan was turning the boat northward, and now they would do battle with the sea.

Listening for his father's laugh to boom, Swift locked his shins against the rail, making himself a part of the ship's pulpit. He carefully let go his grip and spread his arms to the wingspan of a wandering albatross.

With the ship he dove into hollow water crypts, and with the ship he soared, reborn and flying high.

Slipping up and crashing down, through the waves he sailed, ducking his head into rushing eddies of sea air that flushed his lungs with the ecstasy of freedom.

In that frenetic moment, high at the summit of a white wave, Swift was big as any of his brothers.

Justus must be standing on the deck open-mouthed, must be astonished by his mastery of balance.

Swift imagined he could feel his father smile.

"Take the rail, lad," yelled his father. "Three points, keep three points on the ship. Or we'll have you buckled in."

Swift gripped the rail with one hand. He squinted against the low sunlight glittering in the water and blinked back tears summoned by the bite of the maritime wind. He braced as the boat plummeted into a trough.

Trystan mounted the wave, then downshifted the throttle. The sea seemed to settle at the slowing of the boat, and the wind calmed. Trystan steadied the boat's pitch and eased over billows. He pulled into a gentle field of waves.

Euphoric, Swift collapsed against the rail, then dropped flat onto a bench hugging the tip of the bow. He held still for the swelling sun to sponge moisture from his skin, ruddy brown with an aging sunburn, freckled on the shoulders by hours abandoned to exploits in the tangly wood behind his London home.

Warm, dazed, his skin and shorts wicked clean of seawater, Swift tilted his head toward the voices of his father and brothers, tending the sails.

They, more practical in their approach to summer sailing, wore long pants and wind breakers, but not Swift, who was ever topless, his hair a hopeless explosion of dark-blonde tousles.

It was all his mum could do to get him to put on shoes before he'd bolt out of doors, sprung like an animal from a broken trap whenever he'd hear the strange call of a lighting bird, or feel the cool of a coming rain, or spy a bright star rising.

Through slits of crystal-blue eyes, he watched his brothers unfold gear packs, stinking of seaweed and fish skin.

They'd come with rods and reels and tackle and nets, and their business was with the fish.

Swift's business, though, was with the sea.

He looked past them at the oceanic horizon. There was no land in sight—it was just blue on blue with billowing clouds drawing the atmosphere into swirling columns, raising waves and lifting storm petrels. It was just a rippling, indigo seascape that the white plumes of whales might break, and an immediacy of blue-black rolls that dorsal fins might cut.

Swift gathered his knees beneath him and leaned over the rail. While the men fished, he'd scout for monsters—yes, real monsters —that troubled the deep waters, their bellies hungry for blood; their teeth craving the crunch of bones.

Sun-kissed and calm, Swift settled back to lying on the bench. Blood rushing through him felt like swells, like surging ocean currents. It was seawater that coursed in his veins, he tried to believe, making him Poseidon's child. Poseidon was called *the tamer of horses*, and *the savior of ships—the protector of all waters*, and his mortal children were emperors, pirate kings, princes, and bandits. Who wouldn't want to be among them?

Despite how badly he wished to be Poseidon's child, though—a rambler of water worlds, gliding in the company of scaled and slick-skinned beasts—a child of the sea, he'd never be. A child of the sea would ride the backs of white-sided dolphins and green sea turtles, but just keeping his balance on the deck of his father's brigantine was a titan's feat and the best he could probably do.

Swift picked up a shell he'd pilfered from a tangle of sargassum weed, a plaything, maybe, of a real sea child. He held it over his face and toyed with it.

"Swift!" a brother called.

Swift ignored him.

One side of the shell was ragged.

He gripped its jagged rim and tried to break it further.

But the flat cockle was a plate of armor, like the calcified scale of an ocean dragon, and the struggle punctured a hole in his soft finger.

Blood trickled into the curling nose of the shell and dripped onto his chest.

He wiped the shell, painting a sanguine smear on its pearled underbelly.

He studied the naked brownness of himself and the drips of blood bejeweling him. He was soft as a caramel—tender-bodied as a mollusk with no case.

The rocking sea turned the boat a degree or two. Its starboard flank tilted in and out of gentle waves.

Swift rolled over and reached through the rail. He splashed water onto his chest, then dangled his bleeding finger over the edge, letting the lolling of the boat dip it in and out of the sea.

His blood drops sank into the blue current, inciting a liquid magic that would summon creatures of the deep to rise and hunt.

A foot kicked Swift's ankles off the bench.

He tipped and scrambled to standing.

Edric, his biggest brother, stared down. "Come help." He pressed a bundle of gear against Swift's chest.

Swift struggled beneath its weight but kept his hold.

Justus laughed a good-natured laugh; a brawny laugh that keeps fine company with rosy cheeks and white whiskers.

He watched Swift teeter beneath the heavy load. "Good lad. And when you finish with that one, you can come carry your old man's load."

Justus settled on the bench and pulled out his pipe.

Swift glanced over his shoulder and tipped his head in assent. He wobbled down the stairs to the stern.

He abandoned Edric's bulky ropes and rods and nets and tackle onto the wet wood beside the platform where the men would stand, scoping the hunting grounds, snagging fish out of their fluid atmosphere and dropping them into the brackish tub of water that waited in the corner, sloshing with the buck of the tide.

Swift tried not to look at the tub.

Soon it would be stocked, and it always troubled him to see the caught fish there grow sleepy, while molecules of oxygen, few and poor to begin with, dissipated.

But once the fish were cleaned and cut and baked crisp on skewers in the galley—when they weren't fish anymore, but meat instead—he'd perk up and grow wild again and devour them in a pretense of savagery.

Swift pulled himself along the backstay and climbed onto the rail.

He stared at the sky, deepening with Earth's shadow, expanding over a horizon edging a world of profound depths. Inside those depths were creatures who *could* breathe water, and whose muscled jaws *could* break bone shells. It was a realm where anatomically odd animals used stalked eyes to peer at one another from blue caverns; where fanged leviathans brooded, snarling and snapping, eating each other alive.

Swift leaned low against the rail and rested his chin on his fist.

His gaze traveled to the shallow, sunlight zone where shades of fish hung suspended, oblivious that they'd soon be drawn to their deaths.

He wondered whether the caught fish would think themselves victims of alien abduction. He glanced up, half-expecting to see a hook dropping from the clouds with something irresistible on its tip —chocolate coated, maybe, it would be—and he wondered, if the hook did come, would he bite down on it senselessly, the way the fish would, and would he fly out of the sport fishing boat and up to the darkening atmosphere, away, to the faint new moon, where a family of aliens sat in a jumble of ropes and rods and nets and tackle stinking of the skins of boys, laughing heartily together, the alien father puffing on an alien pipe while skillfully drawing Swift's body out of the blue Earth and tossing him into a sloshing vat of moon mud.

Swift blinked his eyes clear of the fantasy and stood straight. He jumped down from the rail and hopped up the steps to the centerboard to retrieve his father's gear. He stopped at seeing that Caius had fetched the bundle and was bringing it.

Caius, the next youngest at twenty-one, set down the burden with care. He stooped and neatened the pile of supplies Swift had forsaken. "You going to fish with us tonight?"

Swift glanced at his rucksack.

Caius lifted a brow as he settled on a stair. He picked up the rucksack and rummaged.

Swift sat beside him and watched him pull out *20,000 Leagues under the Sea*, by Jules Verne. Its cover showed a cartoon ocean, crowded with colorful fish.

Caius held up the book. "Why would you want to read about the water and its monsters, when you're here in the North Atlantic and can fish in the actual ocean?"

Swift shrugged. "I don't like to fish."

Caius thumbed through the pages, worn soft. "I know."

Justus, having finished with his pipe, tapped the railing with it, dumping charred tobacco remnants onto the skin of the sloshing sea, striped pink and golden with the train of the sinking sun. He walked the length of the boat, his adept sailor's gait impervious to waves. He crowded onto the stair between Caius and Swift.

Swift leaned against his father's knee and watched him work.

Justus hummed as he threaded a glassy fishing line through the metal eyelets of his pole, then affixed measured weights using complex knots Swift liked to watch him tie.

Trystan and Edric hung and lit lamps. The oil flames warmed the platform of the stern, spilling yellow light that cheered the teetering boat's wet wood and flickered on the darkening water.

The lamps in place, the two brothers knelt and unfastened boxes of tackle. They laid open shallow bins of ballyhoo and sardines, and twisted open jars of blue runner bits floating in a thin broth of blood and water.

"You in?" Justus raised a brow as he lifted the littlest pole.

Swift shook his head.

Justus had told Swift many times that he was sure he'd like sport fishing if he gave it a fair go. But Swift, squeamish and unsettled by the sight of the catch, flailing in the throes of suffocation on the surface of the sea, wouldn't chance it.

"What, then, will you do"—Justus disassembled Swift's pole—"while I and your brothers fish?"

Swift held up his book.

"Get on then, get on." Justus set aside his own pole, poised and ready for the hunt, and reached for Edric's.

He glanced at Caius. "See he settles someplace safe."

Caius steered Swift by the back of his neck, guiding him up the stairs and along the leeward corridor. When they reached the beam, he heaved Swift to his shoulders.

Swift giggled and snatched at shroud ropes, trying to swing free of his brother's grip. But Caius was quick, and Swift was caught, helpless atop his big brother.

Caius carried him to the bow and deposited him on the bench. He reached into a trunk and lifted a lichen-blue, woolen blanket. He tossed it at Swift.

Swift caught it and spun it around his shoulders.

The scratchy wool irritated the raw place on his chest, but it felt good anyway because it was thick and drew hot blood from his core and pushed it into the tips of his fingers and toes. The blanket visited heat along the surface of his back and belly too, which was heaven, because the sun had gone, and the twilight was bluing and turning cold.

Caius lit an oil lamp and hung it near.

He guided Swift to lie down and pressed a lumpy pillow beneath his head. "You mustn't move from here, all right?" He angled the lamp near and looked down severely at Swift. "I don't mean to fish any boys out of the sea tonight."

Swift nodded.

Caius smiled at him, then disappeared among the sails.

A tremor of gleefulness struck Swift at being unsupervised with the sea.

He stilled his breathing and listened to the splashing of the sleepless water, and to the four faint, merry voices, his father's merriest of all.

He opened his book.

Swift had read *20,000 Leagues under the Sea* more times than he could count. The sea dandled him, book in hand, as he told himself the old, old story. Stars shimmering in the cobalt canopy provided a magical backdrop for the timeworn pages, brown and dingy, dancing in the flashes of the shuttering amber flame.

Swift grew absorbed in reading until a shooting star hooked his eye. The glittery trail of stardust whizzed, smeared, and faded.

That had been a big one.

Swift lowered his book.

There were no lights on any horizon.

There was no moonglow. The boat beneath him was dusky beneath the dun flickering of the lamp. New stars peeked over the sea's wavering plain, their tiny, mercurial points ascending at a clip he could almost perceive.

He thought about the motion of the Earth, rolling in space, until he felt upside down—his body fixed to the boat by just gravity's strong fist. He imagined himself turning with the wheeling Earth, beneath stars, spinning along the worn, invisible rut it plowed around its sun.

Sweat beaded on his palms and temples, and his stomach cramped.

He sat up, shut his eyes, and gripped the bench.

He would not be seasick. The men were never seasick.

He pushed away the wool to let the night wind cool his face and took slow breaths. He closed his eyes and pictured himself turning upright again until the sensation of weightlessness faded. He stood, shaking his limbs, and went to the starboard rail. He leaned his elbows on the wood and watched the east.

The boat slipped easy, its smooth beams slicking through the silky fluid, leaving a trail of gently rippling molten glass. The water was a pane of liquid obsidian, and the canopy of stars was perfectly reflected, the colors of the tiny lights as true on the sea's surface as in the sky.

Swift wished he could be in the water. There, he'd find himself among Poseidon's actual children—creatures who needed no boat; creatures for whom to kill and be killed was no sport, but a matter of shifting winds; a coming and going of the wheel of sun and the ebbing and flowing of tides.

Swift startled at Edric's shouting. The shout was chased by a zipping spin of fishing line zagging into the sea. Swift tried to press away the mental image of Edric's line drawn by the hooked mouth of a frantic fish who thought freedom had been won.

The deception would persist until the fish felt safe, and then its guard would fall, and Edric would know it by the telepathy of the fishing line, and he'd snag the mouth and wrestle the fish into the boat.

The cackling of Edric and the others rose.

The line zipped. And then came the *sploosh* of the fish hitting the water in the holding tank.

Swift focused on the tinkling of the waves washing the sailboat's planks. He didn't want to hear the men laughing at the same moment he knew the fish was suffocating.

He lay down again on the scratchy blanket and picked up his book. He smoothed a sliver of its edge, wrinkling from having shifted into a puddle in the bench's crease. He was almost at the point of losing himself in the old, old story again, when—*sploosh*.

Swift closed his book. He climbed to his knees and looked over the rail, wondering what kinds of fish his father and brothers were catching.

He reached over his head and fingered the netted rope strung from the rigging to the rail. He lifted himself out of his blanket. He stepped over the lifeline and scaled crisscrossing ratlines until he was suspended over the water.

He glanced behind him and listened for voices.

Caius would have a fit if he found him this way, and his father would swat his rear and send him to the berth and make him sleep in the cramped heat by the galley.

There were no footsteps. The spirited voices drifting from the stern were distant.

Swift climbed further out, twisting the ropes around his hands and feet, letting them hold his weight as he peered into the abyss.

The boat hung over a very deep place. He studied the coiling reflection of the constellation Draco, writhing across the inky sea, and wondered if its form marked the body of an actual serpent— an oarfish, maybe, or an electric eel—twining underneath the boat. He sucked his salty lips, considering that there were probably sharks beneath him. There could even be right whales coursing in a docile flote to find food and love, and to birth giant, blue-skinned newborns in the vast expanse of open water. There'd be bluefire jellies here, and thorny seahorses and spiked hagfish. Way down— way, way down—would lurk anglers and devil-fish, clever snipers that used iridescent trickery to dazzle and snare the damned.

A fin flicked the water just inches from the ship.

Swift startled and punched a foot through a gap in the ratline.

He clung, breathless.

He knew, just knew, he could trace the smooth, slithering glide of a long, blue shark an inch below the water's surface.

He untangled his foot carefully, letting his heart slow.

He calculated the odds of actually seeing a shark. There was no doubt they were here, levitating in a murderous night vigil, smelling the blood the men had let in the water, trolling the boat for an easy kill.

There'd be kitefins and blues, and even whale sharks, but to see one would be rare. There were all kinds of rays, and that flash of fin could more reasonably have come from the flat arm of a skate than from the towering dorsal of a blue shark.

But still, he believed it had been a blue.

Swift wondered at the confounding power of the creatures hanging beneath him in the water.

He pictured all of them, all at once, there, as plentiful as the fish painted on the cover of his book—as dense as the multitude of stars spangling the absolute black canopy—breathing water currents and muscling through riptides.

A child of the sea would breathe free beneath the waves.

He wondered whether, if he dove into the abyss, he'd discover he could breathe underwater.

A black swell heaved against the boat, making the ratlines sway.

Swift wanted to hang from his knees and dip his head into the sea. He imagined the sensation of saltwater trickling into the pipes behind his nose and mouth.

The thought summoned a flush of tears, and the onslaught of the ceaseless waves, shuddering the boat, turned his muscles to water.

He tightened his fingers on the ropes. He lifted his gaze away from the sea and focused on the sky, mindfully refreshing his lungs with cold night wind.

He glanced over his shoulder toward the stern. Even men, out here, were weak—very weak—compared to the creatures who could survive the sea.

If Swift tipped into the North Atlantic, just a moment of isolation in the water is all it would take for a current to divide him from Caius' reach. The waters would strangle him, and creatures would tear him limb from limb, reducing him to little blue runner bits in a broth of saltwater and blood.

Here, on the boat, their floating beam of land, equipped with rods and bait and hooks and line, the men were gods. Swift, even, was a god, though he wielded no rod.

Hovering over the water, he was untouchable, his body a constellation of dark-matter embossing a starless shape against the sea: a night angler. But were he to drop, were he to slip into the abyss, he'd lose his invincibility and succumb to the power of the North Atlantic.

For a long time, Swift watched the silken surface, ruminating about the constant current that was shaping the sea into gentle hills. Starlight lilted in his eyes until they stung and his head grew leaden.

The sounds coming from the stern changed from laughing to singing. The boisterous voices bellowed rusty sailors' melodies about Nelson's blood and mugs of ale and Spanish ladies.

The wind picked up, and the sea shivered, as though stirred by the voices of the drinking men. The voices softened and slurred and sang about Fiddler's Green, which told Swift that the second case of beer had come out. The second case of beer meant bed would be soon for the fishermen.

Not wishing to be caught or swatted or sent to the galley, he pulled his way down the ratline like an octopus, arming and legging the heavy ropes. He settled again on his bench.

The wind sheering past him knocked the sails. The clanging strike of metal and the dull beat of canvas on wood added percussive support to the sailors' songs until they blew themselves out. Soon there was nothing but a sleepy breeze and waves licking the sailboat's hull.

Swift opened his eyes to find Caius snugging the scratchy blanket around his sunburned shoulders. Caius roughed Swift's hair, then stumbled to the trunk, gathered his own crude bedding, and dropped to sleep on the forward deck.

Swift slept too, but it was a light sleep, a cold sleep, for the wind had shifted at the dousing of the lanterns, and a fog had rolled in from the north.

In his dream, Swift was in the sea.

The water overhead was in the sunlight zone, clear as crystal, luminous, and warm.

The middle depth, the twilight zone where his body hung, shone hazy where daylight shafted.

The midnight zone waters beneath were a brew of murky darkness and brine.

Swift waved his hands in the blue-brown fluid to feel the current coursing between his fingers.

Fish swam with him: brawny fish with long fins and round, unblinking eyes. The fish suddenly changed and had wings. Their faces resembled faces of men and women, beautiful but strange, with eyes set wide, the bones of cheeks and chins and noses sharp and high.

The faces were gentle, their smiles soft, and a longing lingered in their eyes—a longing not for blood, but for sea minerals and algae blooms, for soaring through light-shafted waters and vanishing inside oceanic trenches.

They hungered to range wide horizons that no man's gaze had ever touched. They thirsted to dip themselves out of the water and into the star-studded atmosphere of the North Atlantic's night, to wonder at expansive, glistening skies of which the vastness of Earth's oceans were a mere echo.

A firm hand shaking his leg roused Swift to the cognizance of daylight.

He rubbed his eyes, the dusk of his dream lifting.

He twisted his waking face toward his father, standing in a glare of sun.

"Come have breakfast, lad."

Swift pushed away the blanket and followed Justus to the galley.

Halfway down the stairs, Swift stopped.

The quarters below deck were tight, and in them he always felt woozy. He felt especially claustrophobic after having spent the whole of the day and the night in the company of the open sea and sky.

Patient, because his father wanted them all together for meals, he choked down queasiness mounding from the absence of the horizon and followed the stairway to its bottom. He forced down lungfulls of hot air, dense and steamy from the searing of fish, and stained brown with the stench of brewing coffee.

His brothers sat on barstools in the middle of the galley, crowding the red laminate surface of a silver-rimmed diner table. Before them lay a plate of charred fish fillets.

Swift rubbed and cracked his lower back.

Caius handed him a paper plate and forked him a thick steak of North Sea mackerel.

Having no place to sit, Swift leaned against the companionway wall, pressing the bottom of one foot against it for support. He picked the meat off the bones with his fingers.

The glaze of sea salt dusting his skin seasoned the fish wonderfully, and he ate all of it.

"You boys want another run before we sail for home?" Justus helped himself to another snowy plank, thick as the muscled ridge rimming his hand.

"Sure," said Trystan, his mouth full.

Edric nodded.

Caius glanced at a red cooler standing in the corner. "We have enough ice to pack another haul."

"Good. Your mum will be pleased." Justus drew his pipe from his pocket and did himself the favor of packing it while his hands were dry and out of the wind. "Mind the sails, would you Caius?" He glanced at Trystan and Edric. "You gents can help me line the rods." Sawing at a hunk of white meat, he arched a brow at Swift. "Care to fish today?"

Swift let go of a brittle rib bone he'd been rolling between his fingertips. He threw his plate into the metal can.

He should say 'yes.' The fishing boat was his father's prize, and sport fishing in the deep sea with sons was the heart of that prize.

Swift had said 'yes' once before, when he was just eight. Fascinated with the complexity of fishing, with its gear and bait and sails and sea weather and animals, he'd eagerly said 'yes.'

The draw on the rod had been a punch of power, and the recollection of the tension in the line at his first catch still incited a twitching thrill in his hands.

Bravely, he fought the foe snared on the line's bitter end for a long time—a deliciously long time—while his brothers hollered and cheered him on, laughing and hanging onto his chest, steadying him in the fray.

Every fiber in his body had strained against the opposition of a creature that seemed to weigh hundreds of kilos—built to fight. Streamlined and all brawn, it tugged the line and bent the rod, and his father thundered joy and clapped him on the back and bellowed, coaching him to give the slack and reel the bloody bastard in!

Finally, when the fish weakened and drifted near the ship, Swift jerked the rod.

With a whip and a snap, the line and sinker flew out of the water with nothing on the hook but a dangling set of fish lips.

His brothers and father, all tipsy on the golden beer, roared laughter, and Swift had laughed with them, unable to process the shock in any other way.

For weeks they all mocked Swift's fish, swimming off somewhere, gumming at worms, making lipless love with lady fish. Swift had to laugh at the jibes. His brothers were hilarious, and anything they did was a riot.

But in private, when he considered the cold truth about the suffering he'd caused, he cried. It was the memory of the muscle of the animal that generated most of his distress. In its own element, the thing had been sheer power. It'd leaped from the water once during the fight, showing itself as long as Swift's leg and thick as his chest.

Swift was no match for that. It would take little more than the lash of a single wave in the high wind to finish him.

So here was the weak boy in the boat with his line and his hook, goaded by his father's zeal and kept from the fury of the sea by his brothers' strong arms. And there was the fish, fighting with all hell and with the desperation given by instinct, muscling back death. And then, there were the translucent lips, gaping from the tip of the hook, babbling a humiliating and hysterical death sentence of starvation to the mighty beast from whose face they'd been torn.

"No, Father."

Justus rose from his stool and clocked his packed pipe against the stove. "Suit yourself." He bit his pipe and glanced at his youngest son. "If you don't plan to work the sea, then you can work the galley."

Justus climbed the ladder, followed by his older sons.

Swift gathered the greasy paper plates and threw them in the can.

He tossed the blackened pans and spatulas into the small sink and ran water to soak them.

He wet a rag, then dropped onto a padded barstool and worked sticky beer rings off the laminate.

An image flashed before his mind—a piece of his dream.

His dream had been crowded down by the bright and blare of morning, but in the stuffy berth, it emerged, bobbing to the surface of his awareness in chunks, like driftwood in a storm's wake.

Swift rested his cheek on the table and rubbed at a dribble of orange juice drying on its metal rim. He closed his eyes to help the impression of his dream come.

The creatures in the sea; the wings that spread from their strong backs; their faces, like peoples' faces, but weird; their long fins streaming.

There'd been no air in his lungs as he swam among them. There'd been no trail of bubbles leaking out his mouth and nose. There'd just been water and water and water; water around him and in him, saturating and collapsing his chest, deadening his weight, drawing him low and issuing him headfirst into a curling deep-sea current.

Swift opened his eyes. His gaze fell on the red cooler in the corner.

He went to it. He opened its lid on a row of dead-eyed fish— the early morning's haul.

The gills on one of them were still reflexively flaring, the dying body frantic to access oxygen molecules frozen in the ice.

A wash of morning wind descended from the deck.

The fresh air was followed by a sickening push of stagnant heat.

It was as though the suffocating fish had absorbed all the cool oxygen, leaving the galley steamy and vacuous—an airless brig of cramped walls closing in.

Swift couldn't breathe.

He sprang for the ladder and tore up it.

He cast himself on the centerboard of the deck. He gulped air and pulled to his elbows. He rolled onto his back and found himself at Caius' feet.

"Hullo, what's happened to you?" Caius set aside the hawser-laid rope he'd been looping. He hooked a strong arm around Swift's chest and lifted him to his feet. "You okay?"

Brimming with the sense of suffocation, Swift couldn't speak. He was a caught fish, unable to feel oxygen in his blood. He didn't look at Caius.

Caius bent near his face and met his eye. "Why don't you sit on your bench and keep a lookout for right whales? We heard on the radio that other boats are seeing them today."

Swift stumbled to his bench and folded his legs beneath him. The morning was sunny and warm, but the wind, still from the north, was chopping the sea into shards. He closed his eyes and let the crisp breeze do the job of breathing for him.

In the black place behind his eyelids, he still felt like the fish.

But in the wind and open air, he was a ransomed fish, thrown back to sea, gliding again in cold water, the delicious dark current closing overhead and strumming his gills with oxygen-rich fluid.

He laid down and watched the water through the rail, seeing nothing but the fresh blue place where fish can breathe.

Sometime later, the voices in the stern rose and roused Swift to sitting. It was nearly noon, he guessed, by the height of the sun. He listened to his father and brothers talking and laughing, then heard the unmistakable *sploosh* of the body of a fish hitting the holding tank.

Bellow… laugh… *sploosh*… congratulations. Bellow… laugh… *sploosh*… compliments. Bellow… laugh… *sploosh*… words of wonder at the size of the catch.

Swift flopped over and tried to listen to the wind. If he concentrated hard, it would drown out everything.

Everything, that is, except… *sploosh.*

Short of breath again, he leaned against his knees.

Those fish in the holding tank were like prisoners of Nemo, locked in the Nautilus, breathing now, but for how long? They were men in an airlock, with blood trickling down their chins from daggers that hooked their jaws. They were men in an airlock, waiting to be clubbed and flayed and gutted and fried and served blackened on paper plates to hungry boys.

Swift's stomach cramped. Saliva gushed into his mouth. He raised to his knees and lurched over the rail, vomiting liquefied mackerel steaks into the stagnant displacement waves foaming at the base of the hull.

Sploosh.

Tears came with the nausea. Swift squeezed his eyes and spilled them out. More tears came yet—tears about the fish languishing in the tank. He let those fall too.

Shaking, he stood, the sunny deck searing his bare feet.

His throat burning with refluxed acid and bile, his ears ringing, he walked insentiently past the galley, past the lofty main and mast, past the flapping sails, and down the steps to the platform at the stern.

Dazed, he found himself standing among his brothers.

Swift's watery gaze followed his father's line, from the tip of the rod to where it terminated, floating atop waves.

He spotted his own rod, lined and weighted, leaning in the corner against the rail, his father's knot deftly holding a hook.

He felt his father's eyes acknowledge him, felt his father smile. It was like he was one of the men.

But he wasn't one of the men. He was a fish.

"Decided to join us, did you?" asked Edric.

Caius studied his little brother. "Swift?"

Swift dropped his gaze to the holding tank. Six fish crowded it, their finned backs arcing from the top of the water, their tails swishing. Justus turned again to the sea and let out more line, propping his foot against a low rail.

A jolt of energy shot through Swift. He plunged his hands into the tank and seized the largest fish, cinching his fingers around its slippery belly.

The creature startled and smacked its body against the tank's wall. It slapped the water's surface, flaring its bony fins broad. Swift heaved the animal out of the tank and hurled it into the sea.

Sploosh.

Justus dropped his rod at the sight of blood coursing down Swift's hands from where the fins had sliced.

Swift didn't see or feel the blood. He saw only the fresh blueness of the water he wanted to give the fish.

He plunged his hands into the tank and clawed out another fish thrashing, fins slashing.

With a *sploosh* it found itself back in the cold, breathable sea. It wriggled away.

"Stop it." Caius, calm and firm, fastened his arms around Swift's.

The water in the tank was dinged with Swift's blood, and the four fish that remained, stunned and wild, twisted in their bloodbath.

Swift fought the confinement of Caius' arms and freed himself. He caught up another fish and sent it back to sea.

Caius snagged him into a bear hug, gluing his arms to his sides.

Swift went limp in Caius' grip, tears dripping from his chin, blood dripping from his fingers.

He was blind with his fit, but sane enough to feel shame at crying in front of his brothers. His stomach, was it not already empty, would have turned itself out right there.

Seasick, he drooped over Caius' arms. His hands burned.

Edric looked at the ripples in the water where the sea had reclaimed the prize they'd won. "You bloody little duffer." He eyed the lilting tub of water and its poor collection of remaining fish, the dusky fluid sloshing. "Those fish were all but gone, you know. You did little but chum the water for the sharks."

Caius threw Edric a sharp look.

"Edric," said Justus, gathering the rods and casting them to the centerboard. "Leave the lad alone." He stared at the small, wounded hands shedding dark drops of blood, staining the platform crimson, but only stared.

Caius held Swift fast with one arm and reached a towel with the other. He mopped the wet face of his brother, wiping it roughly. He held the towel before Swift and clapped his hands together, soaking up blood and seawater.

Loosed from the cuff of Caius' arms, Swift wrenched away and flew up the stairs.

Unable to escape his father and brothers, locked as he was, a prisoner on high seas, he darted past the sail riggings and onto the bow and threw himself against his bench.

He pulled away the towel and looked at his hands.

They were hamburger meat. Diced in more places than he could count. He pulled taut his palms and fingers. They burned white fire. The broken skin parted like gill slits and leaked great drips of blood.

Afraid, embarrassed, exhausted, and nauseated, he gripped the towel in tight fists and wept.

Gentle hands lifted his shoulders. Swift let the hands guide him to sitting.

"May I look?" Caius crouched before him.

Swift gave him the bloody clubs.

Caius unfurled Swift's fingers.

He opened a canteen and poured chilled freshwater over the diced skin.

The water spattering the deck ran red, then pink, and finally clear. He blotted Swift's skin dry, wiping at new beads of blood, gently examining the depth of each slice.

He arched his brow. "Is there anything in that book of yours about going hand to hand with sea monsters?"

He squeezed ointment on Swift's palms and fingers and worked it into the cuts.

Swift wiped his wet cheek on his shoulder.

Caius held the clean hands by their wrists. "These cuts are deep, but they'll heal quickly if you'll let them. I'm going to wrap them. You mustn't use your hands much for a few days."

Swift nodded.

Caius bound and taped Swift's hands, then tucked away his first aid supplies. He sat on the bench and leaned his elbows on his knees. "Now, what was that about?"

Swift glanced at the stern. "The fish are weak in the tank. But they're strong in the sea. I felt weak when they were in the tank."

Caius nodded. "I see."

"Is father angry with me?"

"No." Caius smiled.

"Are Edric and Trystan angry?"

"Well, yes, but they won't be for long. You can let me deal with them."

Swift sat up and peered through the sails at the stern.

He watched his father kneel on the centerboard and wind their gear into packs.

Edric netted the remaining fish out of the holding tank. He clubbed them one by one and laid them aside for gutting. He dumped the tank's rosy water over the rail, lacing the agitated waves with his little brother's blood and tears. Trystan climbed into the helm and set a course for home, taking care to select a smooth trajectory and gentle speed.

When the engine charged to life and the boat shifted southward, Swift tilted against Caius' side.

He glanced at his book.

Caius picked it up.

He wrapped his arm around his little brother and read to him the stories of other men who'd grappled with unbridled waters. Caius' hands, ruddy with his brother's blood, stained sanguine the soft margins of the pages.

Wild as the free fish knifing through water, wakeful as the bright eyes of stars twinkling over the deep, bold as unwavering ocean currents, Swift lost himself in the old, old story of men blazing trails into the vast, uncharted dominion of Poseidon, protector of all waters.

THE END

Thank you, Tim, for leading me into deeper reaches of the writing craft, patiently persisting in your teaching, until I finally see. Thank you, Karen, for calling for even more paint on the page, helping me sharpen my writer's eye.

Thank you, Brian, George, Kristin, Peter, Margaret, and Bill, for reading thoughtfully, dedicating precious hours to visiting the worlds I discover. Thank you to my cherished critique partners for battering my pages with kind correction —a raining down of petals and a sculpting of soft waters. With your support, I write in favorable winds.

Thank you, Kerri, for making believe with me when we were small, and for your unwavering confidence. And thank you, Joanne, for shaking my voice awake, when you told me I was a good writer.

SWIFT'S JOURNEY CONTINUES

ALSO BY TRICIA D. WAGNER

HOW BRIGHT AND HOW TERRIBLE IS THE DAWN

ON THE DAY WE DISCOVER OUR WINGS.

WHEN AN OLD ANGLER PRESSES TEO TO SEEK A GODDESS—THE SEA ANGEL—FOR RESCUE, TEO SETS OUT ALONG BAJA'S WILD COAST TO TEST WHETHER HELP CAN BE FOUND AT THE HANDS OF THE GODS.

TO LEARN THE TRUTH, HE MUST LOOK BEYOND LEGENDS AND SUMMON THE COURAGE TO CHALLENGE HIS PAPÁ.

AND TO REACH FREEDOM, HE MUST TAP HIS OWN STRENGTH, HIDDEN BENEATH WOUNDS LAID BY GLASS.

ALSO BY TRICIA D. WAGNER

A GIRL BRAVE ENOUGH TO DANCE MAY JUST FIND -

GRIEF SINKS AWAY THROUGH THE SOLES OF TAP SHOES.

A DANCER. A CREATURE. A SPIRE-CAPPED AND LONELY BOARDING SCHOOL. **LITTLE GIRL CAN DANCE** *IS A SPELLBINDING TALE TOLD OVER SIX SWEEPING ACTS. TRICIA D. WAGNER'S SIGNATURE STYLE IS ON TOP FORM IN THIS BEAUTIFUL NOVELLA.*

A WONDERFUL FUSION OF POETIC PROSE AND LIMITLESS IMAGINATION PLUNGES YOU STRAIGHT INTO ANDROMEDA'S MESMERISING WORLD.

PREPARE TO HAVE YOUR HEART BROKEN AND MENDED AGAIN IN THIS SHORT BUT STUNNING FABLE.

*-**ELEANOR HAWKEN**, AUTHOR OF THE BLUE LADY AND SAMMY FERAL'S DIARIES OF WEIRD*

ABOUT THE AUTHOR

TRICIA D. WAGNER IS AN AWARD-WINNING NOVELIST, POET, AND SHORT STORY WRITER. SHE GREW UP IN AMARILLO, TEXAS, CHASING STORMS, RIDING STALLIONS, SOJOURNING THROUGH PAINTED CANYONS, DISAPPEARING INTO FLOATING MESAS UNDER STARRY SKIES.

SHE NOW LIVES IN ROCKFORD, ILLINOIS (THOUGH THE TRUTH IS, SHE'S A CITIZEN OF A DOZEN FICTIONAL COUNTRIES). TRICIA WORKS IN EDUCATION AND LIVES DAY TO DAY WONDERSTRUCK BUT LUCKILY CAN FEEL HER WAY ABOUT THIS TERRIFYING, BEAUTIFUL EARTH THROUGH WRITING.

TRICIA HAS PIECES PUBLISHED IN THE *WRITE CITY MAGAZINE*, *CHICAGO NEWA*, *WORD OF ART 3D*, *LITERARY YARD*, AND *MIDWEST REVIEW*.

Author's Note

I love connecting with readers and writers. If, you're interested in stories, then you're a kindred spirit to me, and I have lots more in store for you.

To quote another kindred spirit in writing, Jedi Master Stephen King:

"Writing is magic, as much as the water of life as any other art. The water is free. So drink. Drink and be filled up."

If you're interested not only in stories, but in story creation, visit my website and sign up to receive a **FREE Story Kickoff Character Worksheet.**

I designed this tool for that first moment of getting our feet wet at the brink of a story.

To get your FREE worksheet, visit:
www.TriciaWagner.com